Our Class

by David Parker
Illustrated by Margeaux Lucas

Scholastic Inc.
New York   Toronto   London   Auckland   Sydney
Mexico City   New Delhi   Hong Kong   Buenos Aires

To teachers, parents, and administrators.
— D.P.

To Jim and Karen Lucas and family.
— M.L.

ISBN-13: 978-0-545-00384-1
ISBN-10: 0-545-00384-9

12 11 10 9 8 7 6 5 4 3 2 1   7 8 9 10 11 12/0

Printed in the U.S.A.
First printing, October 2007

Chapter One
Our Class

Room 211

This is room 211.
It's a terrific classroom.
Mr. James is our teacher.
Today, he has a question for the class.

"How can we make our classroom even better?" asks Mr. James.
"Should we use our imaginations?" I ask.
"Of course!" says Mr. James.

"We could have lots of plants,"
says Justin.
"And a class pet," adds Ryan.

"Let's have a place to hang our artwork," says Paige.
"We can put up new pictures every week," says Hayden.

Douglas suggests a reading corner. "It can have baskets of books and comfy beanbag chairs to sit and read in," he says.

"We need a place to do our work," says José. "Can we push the desks together for group reading?"
"Then we can move them back into rows for math," says Alberto.

"We need a desk for the computer,"
says Crystal.
"And a place to keep our school
supplies," adds Hayden.
"We also have to make sure to keep
the room clean," Ryan reminds us.

"We can have a box where we put
new ideas," says Robyn.
"That way we can always be thinking
of ways to make the classroom better,"
I say.

"Can we do all this to our classroom?" I ask.
"It will be a lot of work," Mr. James says with a smile, "but you can make it happen."

Chapter 2
Making a Plan

"You have some great ideas," says Mr. James. "But how will you make them work? And how will you take care of your new classroom?"

"We can divide up the jobs,"
says Abby.
"Some of us can help set up the
classroom," says Crystal.
"And others can keep it clean,"
adds Paige.

"We should each have jobs that work on our own ideas," says Justin. "I can water the plants since that was my idea."

"I don't think that seems fair," says Douglas. "I can't make the reading corner all by myself."

"How about letting people do the jobs they want to do?" asks Ryan. "But everyone might want the same job," Marcus replies.

"We can choose jobs from a bowl,"
says Jennifer.
"I hope I don't pick something hard,"
says Justin.
"What happens if we pick the same
job two days in a row?" asks Paige.
"It won't be fair if we don't take turns,"
Robyn adds.

"This is not easy," I say.
"Finding solutions to your problems can be hard work," Mr. James agrees.

"We can list all of the jobs on the chalkboard," says Marcus.
"And list everyone in the class, too," adds Jennifer.

"Everyone can do one job each week," I say. "The chart will help us keep track. We can take turns with all of the jobs."
"Now that sounds fair!" says Robyn.

Chapter 3
Working Together

"All of the jobs will help the class,"
I say.
"Doing them together will make the
work easier," says Justin.
"And our classroom will be better, so
we can play and learn," says Paige.

"I'm so proud of all of you," says Mr. James. "You've learned a lot about hard work and responsibility today."

"There are many jobs in the classroom," says Abby.
"And we have to share the work to get it all done," adds Justin.

"What happens now?" I ask.
Mr. James smiles. "Let's get to work on our new classroom!"

What jobs can *you* do to make your classroom a terrific place?